Trilogy of
The Boogie Men

Gregory Douglas

PEGASUS BOOKS

Pegasus Books
8165 Valley Green Drive
Sacramento, CA 95820
www.pegasusbooks.net

First Edition: January 2020
Published in North America by Pegasus Books. For information, please contact Gregory Douglas c/o Marcus McGee, 8165 Valley Green Drive, Sacramento, CA 95823.

Library of Congress Cataloguing-In-Publication Data
Gregory Douglas
Trilogy of the Boogie Men – 1st ed
p. cm.
Library of Congress Control Number: 201895357
ISBN – 978-1-941859-78-0

1. FICTION / African American. 2. FICTION / Dark/ Fantasy 3. DRAMA / American/General. 4. DRAMA / General. 5. FICTION / Horror.

10 9 8 7 6 5 4 3 2 1

Comments about *Trilogy of the Boogie Men* and requests for additional copies, book club rates and author speaking appearances may be addressed to Gregory Douglas or Pegasus Books c/ Marcus McGee, 8165 Valley Green Drive, Sacramento, CA 95823., or you can send your comments and requests via e-mail to gregorydouglas1@mac.com.

Also available as an eBook from Internet retailers and from Pegasus Books

Printed in the United States of America

STOCKHOLM BLUE

Sometimes
I think of you
And some of the things you used to do
And then the color fades to blue
And I'm alone again...

This trilogy is dedicated to anyone who has ever had a Boogieman in his or her life. Whether created by others, or borne of your own imaginings, many of us have spent most of our lives trying to avoid, forget about or cope with these "Apparitions of the Darkness."

THE BOOGIE MAN

At six years of age, Bobby feared nothing. He was the man of the house, and his self-confidence was equaled to that of any adult. When his mother left for work at night, this small domain of two bedrooms, a living room, a dinette, a bathroom, and a little brother were all left in his capable hands.

There had been a few mishaps that his mother's keen eyes hadn't overlooked. For instance, sugar on the floor from making "sugar toast" and peas that had met a similar fate while swinging on the refrigerator door. These events had been rewarded with a painful reprimand. Future evidence would never again be detected, no, not even by Sherlock Holmes himself.

Bedtime was always at six-thirty. At precisely seven o'clock it was totally dark in the apartment and Bobby's rabbit ears could hear the deadbolt lock. That's when this six-year-old's freedom began. After checking to make sure that his little brother was fast asleep, Bobby would slowly and painstakingly lift one leg and then the other with just as much control, over the bed until his toes and then his heels silently reached the floor.

Mustering all his effort in patience, he slowly stepped toward the door then turned the knob to open it. Stepping through the doorway Bobby held the knob on the other side until he was rewarded with its silent closure. He then tip toed a few paces past the bathroom and turning the corner, he would bolt down the hallway.

Once in the living room, Bobby would lie on the floor in the darkness and watch the walls as lights from passing vehicles created a beacon, which revolved around the room. It almost seemed like a slow-motion picture show.

After tiring of this, he would stand and find himself no taller than their ancient radio. The on-off volume and tuner switches were the only two out of the eight that worked. He then turned it on and retreating to the floor, Bobby would press his feet up against those monstrous speakers.

He could feel every comma, every period and every exclamation point surging right through his body. Whether it was "Jack Benny", or "Amos and Andy", "Gunsmoke" or others, Bobby's vivid imagination would allow him to be like liquid, filling any vessel that his imagination was poured into.

His favorite program was "The Inner Sanctum" because it took about fifteen minutes to open that heavy, creaky, dark, gargoyle engraved door. Each vibration would rocket right into his spine. His bravery, however, would not allow him to move a muscle or the spell would be broken.

At night when the moon was full, its rays almost lit up the entire living room. After the action shows ended, he would listen to light jazz melodies and soft music. "Two Silhouettes on the Shade" reminded him of the young couple across the courtyard and a floor below them.

Once, Bobby had seen their images projected onto the yellow shade first separate and then drawn together as if magnetized. Once fused, they slowly sank below the level of the windowsill and the lights soon dimmed. Nat King Cole, Frank Sinatra, Rosemary Clooney and others sang on and on, on and on.

"Robert Edward!!! What are you doing up? Boy, I ought to spank you!!!" He had overstayed his welcome. With a voice that spewed dragon's fire his mother had decimated his solitude. She then sent him back to his room with tragedy written upon his face and with pain well etched upon his partially cremated bottom.

These events were occurring far too often for a mother whose frustration level had just about reached the boiling point. She had already felt guilty about leaving Bobby and his brother Steve alone at nights but none of the day jobs that she qualified for would support a mother with two children.

Her concern was for the welfare of both of her children and she was afraid that her "Little Man's" mischief might place both of her children in harm's way. Her solution, however, was every bit as terrifying.

One evening just before departing, she took Bobby aside. "I don't know how you've been so lucky in the past," she explained. "How have you been able to avoid him?"

"Lucky? Him? What's she talking about?" He muttered under his breath.

"Bobby, I'm talking about the BOOGIE MAN!!! He's a big black creature that stands about ten feet tall. He has big white eyes and razor-sharp white teeth. He only comes out at night and he's always silent. Bobby, he chases and eats children!"

He knew that his mother must be kidding but not a smile appeared upon her face, not even the hint of one.

"The BOOGIE MAN loves to sneak up on children in the dark and if he catches you, some kids have never been found. That's why I want you in the bed at night," and then she left.

Three nights passed without incident. On the fourth, his stealth routine past the bathroom was right on schedule. Suddenly when he turned to run down the hallway, something was different. First, it was darker than he had ever remembered.

Secondly, it was so quiet that he found himself holding his breath to hear anything. The silence was only interrupted by the rapid beating of his own heart. Finally, the air in the apartment seemed so thin that Bobby felt himself gasping for air.

He squinted and tried to peer into the darkness. Then as he cast his eyes towards the ceiling – There He was! Those eyes, those flaming white eyes were riveted on him. Bobby tried to swallow to calm himself, but his throat was dry.

His heartbeat quickened and felt as if it would pound right through his chest while the lower portion of his body was stilted and cemented to the floor. He could feel sweat pouring down his forehead and his pajamas were drenched.

Bobby's first concern was for his brother's safety. With all of the strength that he could summon, he used his arms and hands to push one of his legs backwards. The other leg soon followed. But each step backwards however, brought this enormous beast one step closer and as Bobby's steps quickened, so did the BOOGIE MAN'S.

In desperation, Bobby turned and ran. He could feel the BOOGIE MAN's hot breath on his neck. Bobby opened and slammed his bedroom door. He leapt into the bed and threw the covers over his head. Breathing was so hard that it felt as if someone had placed a car on his chest. He waited to catch his breath. There was only one way to know if he or his brother were safe, and so slowly he began to remove the covers to check the room.

Bobby peered through a small slit only to find those glaring white eyes peering right back at him. He had come right through the door! COVERS UP!!! Bobby stayed securely under those blankets until daylight.

The seed had been planted!

Evenings' joyous adventure had become a living nightmare, hell on earth, survival of the fittest. Being the man of the house, Bobby knew that he had to deal with this intruder. For the first time in his life he was truly afraid.

This BOOGIE MAN was huge, and it seemed too strong to be overpowered but maybe it could be outsmarted. The only facts that Bobby had were "OLD BOOGER" only appeared at night and that the covers had saved him.

When evening came, he began leaving all of the lights on all over the apartment. His mother, however, would turn them off before leaving. She had even back tracked a few times to make sure that there was no waste of electricity.

Once, after being discovered, she had asked him over and over again.

"Why?" But his pride would not let him give an explanation.

With each succeeding dark and fearful night, the apartment was becoming more unfamiliar to him. During the days Bobby would pace off the distance between light switches, but in the darkness, he would forget their height. As it was, he had to stand on his tippy toes to trip them. MR BOOGIE MAN became bolder and bolder with each new encounter.

He no longer waited down the hallway, but he camped outside of Bobby's bedroom door. His eyes still glared but now those long razor white teeth were always on display. He didn't have a cavity – no not even a hint of one.

There was no switch in the hallway between his room and the bathroom so at night there was no light. While the security of his blanket was Bobby's greatest friend, his bladder proved to be his worst enemy. He would feel the pressure building like one of the Five

Chinese Brothers who had swallowed the sea. Two seconds from explosion Bobby would open the bedroom door and sprint towards the bathroom. Old BOOGIE was two steps behind and then one behind with his hulking arms about to grab Bobby when CLICK - LIGHTS ON!!! Ecstatic with his victory, Bobby jumped up and down almost wetting himself.

After relief he discovered how hollow the victory, only half of the course had been covered. And so he waited and waited and waited and he waited.

Finally, it was time. With sweaty palms and his heart racing and about to burst, He leapt out of the bathroom in a full gallop right pass the startled child eater.

Bobby sped through the cracked door then leap frogged over the bedpost and scrambled under those covers – HOME FREE HOME!!!

This monstrosity of terror and ugliness also had a brain and he learned from his mistakes. Bobby, on the other hand, was running out of diversions, detours and deceptions. As a result, his territory was getting smaller and smaller.

Just before nightfall, Bobby would roll up his window shades to allow as much light as possible to enter his room. On nights when there was none, "OLD BOOGER" would stay crouched like a vulture on Bobby's bedpost, and Bobby would stay under the covers.

He would use a broomstick to pitch a tent so that although cramped, he could maneuver. His bladder would remind him of their nightly appointment and after further urging and even demanding relief, alas nature's call would have to be answered.

"Robert Edward Banks! Not Again!" For the past few months Bobby's mother thought that he was regressing. He had begun to have so many "accidents" in his bed. Was he becoming jealous of his little brother, Steve and seeking more attention?

She never noticed however that Bobby's pajamas were never wet or that the evidence was never in the center of his bed. Many years later he got over the "BOOGIE MAN", at least that BOOGIE MAN!

Sam Sam, the Boogie Man

He just appeared one day. Sam, if he had a past history, had not volunteered it, nor had anyone asked him. It was evident by his dress and behavior that Sam was a transient. He would spend most of his time in garbage cans, which he mined like a prospector who had hit the mother lode. He was like a trapper who routinely checked his lines.

Often the seat of his pants was the only visible part of him, as he dug through the garbage cans. Bobby couldn't say that the old man had eaten out of the trash, but some did. His shopping cart was always stacked about a story high with flattened cardboard boxes, cans, newspapers and rags.

Sam was ebony black. He was so black that only once did Bobby see the whites in his eyes and they were blood shot brown. Sam's heart appeared to be every bit as black as his skin. He wasn't very tall and without his cart, his poor posture, with a bowed back and forward lean, made it appear as if he were still pushing an imaginary one.

Sam always wore an overcoat with swatches of cloth and candy wrappers bulging from the pockets just like those of the fraying vest he wore underneath. His oversized plaid pants tallied wrinkles for every day he had been alive and even when rolled up, they still were trod upon. Frequently his shoelaces were untied or missing.

On several occasions, Bobby had seen the old man resole his shoes with old newspaper. The last trace of his former self, perhaps, was the moth-eaten weather worn fedora that he wore.

It actually may have mirrored his life. Sam drank and the whiskey odor clung to him like a frightened squirrel to a tree. It was then that his posture and stride became as exaggerated as a clown inept at balancing a ball on his nose. His words slurred and quite often he would curse at anyone or anything around him.

"Look at that old man over there, he looks like he's walking in an earthquake" whispered Bobby. He, his brother Stevie and a few of the other kids were on their way to the playground one day when they first saw this "oddity" emerging from the alley. When

Sam's cart started zig zagging uncontrollably with him down the sidewalk side swiping the building, his hat tipped to the side and their curiosity only intensified.

"You kids are so nosy. Mind your own business and stop your damned staring," he blurted out. "Ain't you got nothing better to do?"

He then became momentarily preoccupied with an old necklace that he had just plucked from his jacket pocket. Sam attempted to appraise its value by holding the "diamonds" toward the sunlight.

"Damned glass," he cursed, "and damn you nosy kids" he yelled, turning... towards them.

"You're an ugly old man, you look so ugly, you look so ugly that you look just like an old boogieman," shouted Stevie from across the street.

"Boogieman huh," spouted the drunken old man, "and let's see if this will scare you snotty-nosed kids!

He then heaved a coke bottle and lurched at them. Glass splattered everywhere and the now terrified children ran yelling and screaming back to the safety of the stoop. That's how Sam, Sam, the Boogieman had gotten his name.

Sooner or later everyone sat on the stoop. In the morning, from eight thirty until about three thirty in the afternoon, it would serve as a nursery school as well as the crossing guard station.

"Gerald, get out of that street. Boy, what is wrong with you? Are you crazy? You'll get killed running between those cars, and if you don't stop, I'll tell your parents."

These warnings rang out from the stoop with all the clarity of a police siren. If they were not heeded, positive reinforcement arrived that evening in the form of a strap.

The midmorning breeze that shuffled between the apartment buildings was the only source of air conditioning.

"Child, it's going to be some kind of hot today." Mrs. Gordan had already staked her claim to the "Stoop". Even a hint of breeze would serve as a welcomed substitute for the stagnant, oppressive apartment air.

"Yes, girl, it should be a housewives' holiday at the beach today," replied Ethel Jones, who was rocking her three- year-old daughter, Alice. "By mid-afternoon, that apartment is so hot, that you could fry the chicken on a windowsill. And you know that kind of heat's disastrous to my sensitive complexion."

"Well, just put some flour on yourself missy, and you'll cook up just as good as those tough old birds we brought from the market last week," laughed Mrs. Alberta Range as she, too, was setting up shop.

"That's fine for you old birds, but what about me?"

"Gracie Gordon, Huh! Those five kids of yours clipped your wings a long time ago. You can't fly. As a matter of fact, you look more like a roasting hen then a fryer!"

Mrs. Pearl Banks had just arrived. She welcomed the banter between these women, whom she had watched grow since childhood. She knew all about their lives. A willing ear could always capture their happiness and heartaches for they were as free with their histories as the wind.

It added to Mrs. Pearl's otherwise dull existence as a housewife. She looked at little Alice and felt but tried to hide her embarrassment.

Two days earlier, she had baby sat for Mrs. Jones. Little Alice at age three was very impressionable. That morning in the bathroom, as she was washing, Mrs. Pearl had lifted her face from the sink to find little Alice lifting hers from the toilet bowl! Alice was immediately instructed on the proper time and place to wash.

She had thought about revealing this to her mother but her over-riding guilt of having missed little Alice, for even a second, resulted in her silence. Besides, secrets aren't truly secrets, unless they're shared by no more than two. For a few weeks thereafter, she would feel a "hot flash" when little Alice appeared.

Mrs. Pearl had a heart as large as all of out-doors. She was Bobby's grandmother and took him and his brother in without the slightest hesitation when their mother passed away. She was one of the kinder truant officers on this beat.

She was opinionated and strong in her conviction to serve; but because of a stroke, she retained poor eyesight, a very noticeable limp and a very weak voice.

Seeing the children running around the corner like a stampeding herd of wild horses caused a great deal of chaos on the stoop that day. Bobby sprinted around the corner, then skipped three stairs at a time to reach the top of the stoop. As he furiously struggled to get through the masses, Bobby almost fell when his grandmother restrained him.

"Robert Edward Banks! What in the world has gotten into you? You could break your neck coming up those stairs like that!"

He strained to hear her in the confusion and somehow took a deep breath and found his voice. "Grandma, It's Sam, Sam, the Boogieman! he blurted out, trying to loosen himself from her grip. She drew him even closer until they were eye to eye.

"What is all of this about? Are you in trouble? And who is this Sam, Sam, the Boogieman?"

It was at about that time that Bobby looked over the banister and saw the flattened cardboard boxes stacked about two stories high, coming around the corner. The shopping cart pulled to a stop at the edge of the stoop as an old man, reeking of alcohol, was now flailing at the crowd with a half-broken coke bottle.

"That's him Grandma!" Bobby exclaimed as he pulled her towards the door – with lawn chair in tow.

Now calm can reign within a riot just as calm exists in the eye of a storm. And so it was on that day when hobbled but confident Mrs. Pearl, rose from her chair. She stared directly into the eyes of the enraged haggard old man, with cut glass within arm's length of her, and calmly spoke in a voice that was barely audible.

"Mr. Sam, you have had too much to drink. Can't you see that you're scaring our children? It would be better if you just went home and rested."

The sobering effect of these words could be seen upon his face. It was as if he had been awakened from some deep hypnosis. His facial expression changed. The snarled jagged rotten toothed scowl gave way to a confused, warped and drooping face. His shoulders slumped and the jagged coke bottle came to rest at his side.

He slowly turned almost in a complete circle and then looked toward the ground as if he were finding his footing just after an earthquake. Then in total silence, he left. For about three weeks Bobby's grandmother reigned as the local hero. She never said much about it and appeared almost embarrassed by its mention. Sam, it seemed, had just disappeared.

Bobby was awakened each morning by the smell of bacon, eggs and coffee. His grandfather, the head of the family, would always separate himself from the other family members at this time. He would play with "Tweetie," his parakeet.

"I'd like my eggs poached this morning, and don't break the yolks this time", he barked to his wife.

Although she had received a hero's status on the stoop it was business as usual in Grandpa's house. She never seemed insulted by his abrasive remarks.

"Are you going to eat in the kitchen or the living room?" she would reply.

"Now you know I always need to see the morning news, woman! Bring my food into the living room."

There he would sit stroking Tweetie, saying, "pretty bird" while watching the news, until Tweetie had repeated the chant.

"Pretty Bird Tweet Tweet"

"Pretty Bird Tweet Tweet"

Then they would share his breakfast. Tweetie, however, remained a vegetarian. No greater love ever existed between a man and his bird than there was between Grandpa and Tweetie. The bird was a natural charmer and who could resist a bird that would perch upon your shoulder and sing.

Once Grandpa had fallen asleep and Tweetie lit upon his lower lip to peer inside and discover the origin of primitive sounds.

"There's Grandpa snoring again, Grandma. How does he hold his breath so long? Was he a great under water swimmer?" Stevie always had a million questions and loved to play an equal number of pranks.

"Boy you've been up under me all day. Why don't you go to the door and peek into the living room and tell me how your grandfather holds his breath so long." She was finishing up the dishes and wanted to enjoy her first sign of peace and quiet that day. She watched her grandson lean around the corner and look into the living room.

"Grandma, Tweetie is sitting on Grandpa's lip!" whispered Stevie as he turned to face her.

"That bird's doing no such a thing."

"Yes, he is, and now he's looking down Grandpa's throat!" He was now peeking back into the living room.

"Stevie if you continue to tell fibs...."

"But Grandma, I'm not fibbing." Ah, OOOOOh!

"Grandpa just swallowed Tweetie!"

"Boy I'm gonna spank you...."

"But Grandma, he just did. Come and see..."

"Augh, Augh, AUGH!" Cough, cough, COUGH!

"Dern bird," cough, "You could have killed us both." Grandpa had gasped.

"See, I told you so Grandma!" replied Stevie, who had never moved to assist his poor gagging grandfather.

Mrs. Pearl was beside herself. She hadn't believed her grandson, but the gasping and coughing confirmed that he was telling the truth. She arrived as quickly as she could, finding Grandpa and his wet and half balding companion consoling one another.

The incident left Grandpa in a rather foul mood. He had coughed up Tweetie easily enough, but the sensation of feathers and feet in his throat lasted for about three days. This resulted in poor Tweetie's incarceration for about a week.

This parakeet was unflappable. He seemed to feel a peculiar sense of relief from atop his various perches and persisted in decorating shoulders and sometime heads with baubles of a biodegradable nature. Tweetie was truly the smallest bombardier in U.S. Air Force's history.

He flew many missions and was finally lost in action one day when his flight plan took him far off course. It could never be proven, but many thought Grandma [in a less than a Christian mood and with the devil as her fulcrum], had given Tweetie his "window of opportunity".

Grandpa looked for that bird for five months. He would call and even leave the window open at night in anticipation of Tweetie's return. No letter, however, was forth coming from the U.S. Air Force in regards either to the recovery of an MIA or a "We regret to inform you..."

For Bobby, there truly was something very special about being twelve years old. Every day seemed to bring something new. First, a growth spurt had left him five feet and ten inches tall. His parents and friends seemed to have a new regard for him.

Secondly, playgrounds now gave way to bowling alleys, beaches, amusement parks and the movies, with less parental guidance. And lastly, the word "girlfriend" began to hold more appeal. There was a sense of independence and his growing confidence stemmed from his progress in sports.

Bobby could run, jump, bat, catch and throw with the best of them. When sides were chosen, he'd never be taken less than second, that is with the exception of one sport: roller-skating.

Everything else in his life was a glowing triumph, but his roller-skating was an abysmal failure. "Swing your arms and move your feet. Push off from the inside." Linda had become an almost constant companion. Her instruction prompted him to try. Try, Bobby would try. Fail. Bobby would fail.

When he tried to go forward, it almost looked as if he were trying to stand still. In order to get up the long Centre Avenue hill, he would have to hold fast to the building's bricks in a hand over hand fashion and snowplow his way to the top. The six and seven-year-old kids looked like professionals as they roller-skated rings around him.

"How can you run so fast and roller-skate so God awful poorly?" asked his grandpa one evening from the stoop. "Your legs look like wet noodles in a windstorm."

Grandpa shook his head and seemed almost embarrassed for his grandson who was dubbed "the worst skater on the block." Bobby prayed and God, at least in Bobby's estimation, unfailingly showed his sense of humor. For no matter how hard he tried, he simply didn't improve. But he never gave up.

The summer rolled on into a hot and humid August. "Today's forecast calls for the century mark, with seventy percent humidity. The time now is seven thirty, and its seventy-six degrees on W.B.R.D..." blared the television in the living room as its only occupant stared out of the half-cracked window.

It's going to be a scorcher today. Is my breakfast ready yet? What could take so long? It's just eggs and toast." Grandpa, in spite of everything else, had not lost his morning edge. At ten o'clock on Saturday parents and children alike began filtering out of their apartments and onto the stoop and streets to find a cool breeze blowing between the buildings. By midmorning the taller apartments served as shade for the smaller buildings. The girls had already taken up the sidewalk. "Five, ten, fifteen, twenty..." Began the cadence of each double-dutch turn.

"We got here first. Na, nanah, nahnah, nah." sang Wilma.

"Wilma the whiner, we'd love to give you a shiner." chanted Barry Sampson. He couldn't stand her or her hopscotch. The girls were determined not to share their staked-out turf.

A shouting match between the sexes then followed and caught the attention of the stoop guardians.

"We don't understand why you children can't get along. Why don't you play something that all of you can play?" Mrs. Wood always sought a compromise."

"What about hide and go seek?" asked Bruce.

"Man, we played that last night and I'm tired of it." answered Lee.

"What about a double-dutch championship?" asked Sarah.

"Nah, you girls always win that and it's no fun," replied Michael.

"What about a roller-skating contest to determine the Champion of the Whole Block?" suggested, of all people, Bobby. It was just a way to put his two cents into the conversation and besides no one would ever fall for that idea, he thought.

"Alright!" What a great idea! We can call it The First 'Around the Block Roller-Skating Championship' because no one had ever thought of it before. That was the best idea you have ever come up with. It's pure genius", said Linda. Bobby felt good every time Linda spoke to him because he liked her a lot.

Every kid on the block left to get their skates. The news was spread from window to window and down the hallways, that the championship of skating was being put on the line today. The day had been transformed into a carnival atmosphere. Moms, dads, aunts and uncles were now littering the stoop in order to get a good view of the race.

Some mothers were leaning out of their windowsills with babies securely tucked under their arms like loaves of bread. One lady had even set up a Kool-Aid stand on the stoop. Sale: One cup for a nickel.

"This isn't fair. We little kids want a chance to win, too" complained Marilyn, one of the smartest seven-year-olds that anyone ever knew. "How are we going to make this fair for the little kids?" Mrs. Pearl in her infinite wisdom had the answer and signaled the children to gather around.

"The little ones should be given a twenty-yard head start." Her loudest voice always sounded like she was hoarse. "That way the race will be fair, and the youngsters won't get trampled at the start."

"That seems fair enough." said Chubby Foster, unable to conceal the smile on his face.

"No. It's not fair." complained Bobby. "Chubby Foster, you know that you're one of the faster skaters on the block. You should be in the back."

"That doesn't matter. We're doing this by age. Why are you so worried? Do you need to be up front?"

At first, the other children stared at Bobby and then, as if on cue, started smiling as laughter then filled the air. The older kids were leaning over the banister with tears in their eyes.

"We'll let you get up front too." They said. Bobby put his pride in his back pocket and towering over the youngsters, took his position in the front line.

Since the apartments were situated on a hill in catty-wampus fashion, the first two legs of the racecourse were downhill. The third leg was perfectly flat, and the last leg was the all-uphill Centre Avenue.

The parents were yelling encouragement from stoops and windows. As Mr. Ball raised his hand, silence reigned. "Are you ready? On your mark! Get set! Go!" he shouted.

The screeching of skate wheels on the pavement sounded like a car braking just before an accident – they were off! Bobby had been blessed with his best start ever. This kept him dead even with the fastest of the younger kids, and he was feeling good.

At the end of the first leg, the stagger had been made up. Bobby had taken the first turn wide and had almost hit a parked car on the other side of the street.

"Mr. Molasses lets everyone pass us. Get out of the way big brother," shouted Stevie. He became the tenth or eleventh kid to zip by Bobby.

By the third turn, Linda seemed to have taken control of the race. Bobby remained undiscouraged as the world, skaters and snails alike, passed him. When he finally reached Centre

Avenue, he knew that someone had already won, but he just wanted to finish.

As he started up Centre Avenue, Bobby's progress slowed. He swung his arms and legs faster, but he found himself at a standstill on the uphill grade.

"I'm going to finish this if it's the last thing I do. I have never been completely around this block but I'm going to do it today. Just one step at a time. Just one step at a time," he continued repeating to himself and with each repetition he could feel himself getting one step closer to his goal.

He held fast to the bricks of the building using his hand over hand, snowplow technique and for all its awkwardness, he knew that he could make it. Bobby looked toward the finish line; about sixty yards away and actually heard friends cheering him on.

Across the street, not too far from him, two stories high worth of cardboard boxes in a shopping cart emerged from the dark alleyway. Screams rang out from the hilltop. "Run Bobby Run! It's Sam, Sam, the Boogieman!"

Bobby turned to see the old man appearing from behind his loaded down shopping cart. His confidence left him as fast as water leaves an overturned glass. He tried to run, then fell. He then got up and fell again. Then he started crawling. Seeing the old man now crossing the street, Linda skated to his defense.

"Sam, Sam, the Boogieman, you better leave him along!" she screamed as she approached him. Sam charged towards her, hurling a bottle in her direction.

The glass shattered a foot in front of her but ricocheted off the pavement and cut her leg. Blood started streaming from the glancing wound as if an artery had been severed. Now scared and wounded, she skated back towards the stoop crying hysterically and yelling, "Sam, Sam, the Boogieman just cut me!"

The old man was now hovering over Bobby, like a buzzard investigating a carcass. Sam then looked towards the crowd at the top of the hill.

"Leave me the hell along. All of you, just leave me be. No Respect, No Respect, No Peace..." and heaved a bottle at them. Then turning towards his prey, he extended his hand.

"Take my hand."

In total disbelief Bobby gazed into the face under that weather worn fedora and saw compassion in this old man's face. As he extended his own, Bobby realized he and Sam were building a bridge over the abyss of misunderstanding.

They were just an old man and a young boy whose paths had crossed a few times and whose actions, in the past, only represented a shadow of the person, not the person himself. It was like the tip of an iceberg. The youngster now realized the old man's cursing and bottle throwing, [which was always short of the mark], were his only means of defense.

Bobby was helped to his feet and found Sam's hands to be as coarse as tree bark. He was strong for such an old man, yet gentle in his assistance. As they took the measure of one another, their silence was shattered. Some of the stoop guardians grabbed Sam, took him back into the alley and beat him.

"Don't hurt him. Please don't hurt him. He doesn't mean any harm." Bobby's pleas to help the old man seemed no louder than his grandmother's voice as cheers rang out for each blow delivered and drowned Bobby out. He then realized that differences are manifest with alarm and hatred while similarities are manifest with acceptance and kindness. It seemed, to Bobby, the human rule but not the humane thing. As for Sam, Sam, the Boogieman, he was never seen or heard from again.

Where Boogie Men Dare

The strobe light splintered the darkness and splashed silhouettes onto the walls as it revolved around and around. As the night wore on, the "Philly Dog' surrendered to Otis Redding's "I've Been Loving You Too Long, I Don't Want to Stop Now".

"Sir, Sir! You're dancing far too close to that young lady. Certain standards must be met here. If not, I'm going to have to separate the two of you."

"What do you want me to do, dance at arm's length? "was the response.

This marked the third time that Robert Banks had to issue this warning and he was now warming to his task as chaperon.

"Sir, just one more time, Sir," and Bobby pointed towards the door. After a brief silence, laughter erupted between the couple and this first-time chaperon. In the 1960s, "Father/Daughter Weekend, was a tradition at most Historically Black Colleges, and signaled the start of "Spring Break."

Bobby, now a junior, was on the top of the world. From a walk ~ on freshman in football he had earned a full scholarship. After completing his midterm exams earlier in the day, he felt sure that he hadn't tarnished his 3.8 G.P.A.

He was selected for and reluctantly accepted the job of chaperone with a few other students for the Father/Daughter

Event. Now, seeing the co-eds and their fathers enjoying themselves so much, he was glad that he had.

"Mr. Banks, I certainly enjoyed the way that you chaperoned this evening", remarked

Reverend Littleton Lowe, "and if you have the good fortune to date my daughter, well, I'm hoping that you will hold yourself as accountable as you have held me."

"Rev. Lowe, what I will remember is those smooth moves you threw down on the dance floor. Is that something you picked up at Divinity School?" Bobby smiled.

"Mr. Banks, as you may or may not know, I also attended this institution of higher

Learning. As a matter of fact, I had to teach some of my classmates some of the finer

points of ..." Reverend Lowe pulled up his slacks and shuffled his feet across the floor with the precision of the "God Father of Soul". Bobby's mouth dropped and not a word

fell out.

"Daddy, you're embarrassing me again", said Lillie Littleton, attempting to drag him to the door. He momentarily resisted. "Mr. Banks, a man may come from any of several backgrounds", he started, and on his journey the trials and tribulations that he endures serve as the tools to tune up his character. Using this to the best of your ability and sharing his best with others, creates a man among men. Either way it doesn't mean that you can't get down on the dance floor."

Reverend Lowe then smiled, winked, flashed a peace sign and left with Lillie in tow. The party continued until midnight and by that time, there wasn't a father that Bobby hadn't met.

Uninvited sunlight slithered between the windowsill and the venetian blinds to pierce slumbers darkness. Bobby got up, showered, dressed and headed toward the cafeteria.

"Thought that you were something last night, didn't you Mr. Banks?" As he turned there was Sheila about three feet away. She approached and gently tugged on his ear. She loved to tease him and who couldn't accept ribbing from Sheila?

Sheila was at the top of her class but before you could ever get to academics you had to get pass her breath-taking beauty. Her perfect eight-inch afro framed her gorgeous smile while her olive brown complexion enhanced those piercing hazel eyes and that M&M body melted in your mind at the "id level."

At 5'6," she walked with the grace of a Nubian princess, head and shoulders always erect and those arms swinging as gently as the willows when they responded to zephyrs. Bobby doubted that her shoes ever touched the ground, but he had never actually noticed her shoes.

The yellow tank-top that she now wore covered the subject of so much speculation and her daisy duke cutoffs gently draped the crease of her buttocks whose mounds

"You've got me going in circles..."

"Ahem, Mr. Banks, cat got your tongue?"

"Sheila, why do you want to mess with me? You know that I was up late last night?"

They walked together.

"You paraded around that dance worse than my father. As a matter of fact, after watching you, I found a new respect for my father." That's what these affairs are all about, respect" he replied and with more sincerity than Sheila was used to from him.

"Sometimes you seem too serious. Sometimes when I'm with you it seems like you go off into a world of your own. I don't know what goes on in there, but I wait for you to emerge." She placed a sisterly arm around his shoulder, but Bobby remained reluctant to let her in.

"Hopefully it's for the better. I've had a lot on my mind."

For months now Bobby had agonized over the prospect of losing a friend by revealing his true feelings for this remarkable woman. He had tried once before but in the middle of his declaration he lost his nerve, perhaps because of the constant interruptions from friends.

Bobby had guessed that he was obviously light years further down the road in the relationship then she was because if she felt the same way, well there was no indication.

They had gone through the cafeteria line without a word and were now seated.

"There you go again. Bobby, oh Bobby! Where are you?"

"I'm right here with you. Trying to get through these delicious powdered eggs and prefabricated ham that my granddaddy must have slaughtered fifty years ago. It tastes like it. Doesn't it?"

Sheila had decided to give Bobby his space. There was definitely something on his mind, but she decided not to pry. She had like him from the first day that they had run into one another. Late for football practice, Bobby had taken the short cut between the library and Harriet Tubman Hall. He hurtled the three-foot shrubbery successfully but was unable to avoid the startled coed on the sidewalk. Books and papers were scattered over half of the campus.

Wounded prides were quickly mended, and their friendship was immediate. She was intrigued by his drive both on and off the field. They became close friends; study partners and each other's shoulder to cry on when affairs of the heart soured. In the past three weeks she had noticed when Mr. Banks appeared her gaze labored upon him uncomfortably long, but no.

"Sheila, when are you going to give someone else a chance? I think you're trying to smother Mr. Bobby Banks so you can keep him all to yourself," remarked Kim.

"I have no chains on the man, Kim, if you're interested, talk to him." Kim had been teasing Sheila for eight weeks about Bobby and this had been the stock reply that she had delivered without a thought. Lately, however, she had become irritated about the question and very sensitive about the man. As Sheila reappeared from her "own world", she realized that she had been staring at Bobby the entire time. They continued to eat in silence that morning and then each went their separate way.

With such a beautiful Saturday before him, Robert Banks decided to commit "the crime of the Century" and clean his room. He knew that his industry was fueled by the thought of Sheila.

One of his biggest problems just like with her, was his procrastination. He decided to turn over a new leaf and made a new resolution: "Not putting off today the problems that you can solve today". Gosh that sounded good and so simple but following through with it – that was his biggest stumbling block.

He mopped and waxed the floor, took out the trash, cleaned out his closet and draws and even polished his shoes until he could see his face in them. His room was spotless, and he was proud of himself.

He then started his trek to the cleaners off campus. Mid-term exams had been completed and the Kappa's, the Alphas, the Omegas, the Sigma's, and the Grooves would all be partying heavily tonight. Now Bobby could fraternize, he could dance, he had no problems speaking to the opposite sex (with one exception), but he couldn't drink.

He liked the little lift that it gave him but what he didn't like was the consequences of excess. How much was too much? This became his little science project. A few times

the experiment had blown up in his face and more than a few times all over his clothes as he continually called out for but never saw a guy named "Earl." Ike, Bobby's best friend had suggested another project like perhaps drinking Seven-Up or Coca Cola for reasons of sobriety and preserving undamaged brain cells.

The walk to the cleaners on that April 17th was accomplished in ninety-degree weather with eighty percent humidity. The twenty-dollar bill he placed on the counter quickly shriveled up to a dollar and nineteen cents.

Now hot, dejected and broke, Bobby headed back to the campus with both arms loaded down with cleaning. His hands were drenched with sweat and the shirts kept slipping from his grasp.

"Darn it! If you weren't so lazy you should have made two trips." He was chastising himself for such poor planning, but his torment was just beginning.

"Why didn't you ask Sheila to help? You know that she would have. Maybe you could have told her how you feel? After all, how far could she go on foot, loaded down with half of my laundry? Maybe she..." BEEP! BEEP!

Bobby hadn't noticed that a 1967 dark blue Buick Riviera had been beside him for the past twenty seconds. The tinted window on the passenger side rolled down.

"Can I help you, young fellow?"

"Yes, Sir. I'm going back to campus, Thank You."

"Well just throw your clothes in the back and I'll have you there in no time."

And so Bobby did. He jumped into the passenger's side of the car and was relieved to find the comfort of air conditioning.

"What a great car. It must be brand new."

Yes, it is. How did you know?"

Any male his age that had walked this town for two years definitely knew every new car on the market, Bobby thought to himself.

"Oh, I haven't seen many Riviera's, sir. Just in the magazines."

The smiling middle-aged man looked every bit the image of one of the fathers from the dance, but Bobby couldn't put a name to the face. Last night, the strobe light had only revealed fragments of faces and his brain had created a montage.

"You're a very observant young man. You know, you look like a football player. Would you like to see what she can do?' Mr. X asked.

"You're pretty observant yourself. I'm a defensive halfback" Bobby comfortably volunteered, "and I'd love to see what she can do."

After they had raced down Main Street without so much as a shimmy or a ticket, Mr. X pulled over and they laughed about it.

"Son, I like you. How would you like to go with me to a party? There will be lots of booze and women?"

Bobby had taken a liking to Mr. X, who obviously had a host of friends that were ready to get the party on at eleven forty in the morning.

"Sure. But the women are yours; I wouldn't mind a little booze, though". Where's the party?

"In the West End" was X's reply.

Now Bobby had only been in the West End once before, two years ago to a house party, and Ike had to drag "Mr. Dead Weight" home. But that was two years ago.

As they continued, the estate type homes with carefully manicured yards and avenues gave way to two-way traffic on one-way streets. Garbage cans began to litter the sidewalks and half clothed children played in them.

Some of the houses were boarded up. In this neighborhood, the paint was so visibly-cracked that the houses looked like unfinished jig saw puzzles. Weeds infested yards; gaping cracks in cement sidewalks, and porches without banisters as well as broken or missing steps validated the severe poverty and total neglect of the area. It appeared almost primitive.

"Man, we're gonna have a good time! And don't worry. I'll get you back to the campus."

Mr. X continued to talk in run on sentences about the women and the booze at the party. This first presentation of incongruous clues now put Bobby in a toned-down mood.

"Where is this guy taking me? Brand new Riviera in this neighborhood?" Bobby's subconscious was trying to send him a wakeup call but his preoccupation with this party wasn't letting enough sunlight in to burn off the fog.

"How much further is it?" He knew that his rising anxiety had not been masked. "It's just in the next block." Mr. X's reply seemed a little strained, but he continued to joke in spite of it.

I gave Earl forty dollars for the booze, so I know that there's plenty of booze left." The car pulled up to the curb.

"Let's get this party going right!"

Bobby had anticipated laughter and music but was met with dead silence as he emerged from the car. It was the first time that Bobby had seen Mr. X stand. In the car he had assumed that Mr. X was average height but now standing he was clearly 6-feet three-inches" of Paunchiness. Bobby estimated he weighed about two hundred and forty pounds.

"Where's the party?" He was truly nervous now. In researching his memory, he had once again failed to identify this suspected father from last night's dance.

"Ah, they're probably out in the back yard. Come on, you'll see," exclaimed the jovial Mr. X.

As they climbed to the top of the steps of the decrepit porch, Bobby was asked to wait because Mr. X. had forgotten to lock the car doors. Upon his return, "Go right on in. The party's right upstairs Bobby."

There now seemed an urgency in X's voice and where a big smile had once graced his face, there was now just half of one. Bobby opened the door and a loud creaking sound could be heard from the rusting hinges that hadn't been oiled in fourteen years.

He needed no large speakers for these vibrations were coming right up from the floor and through his shoes. His memory had unwittingly flashed back to age six.

Once the door closed, silence reigned inside. There was no visible light source in the hallway, which was as dark as the blackest of nights. His heart instantly raced to two hundred beats per-minute. His pulse was being counted out on his eardrums and drowned out everything but the exhumed fear of a six-year-old boy.

Now drenched, he could feel sweat pouring down his legs in rivulets. It was then that the conclusion had finally hit home: Mr. X was not a friend, but an old fiend, who had come home to roost once again.

This, however, was not the silent apparition of a six-year-old, or a defensive, bottle throwing, bourbon breathed old man. Bobby's brain commanded his stilted legs to move faster in order to separate himself from the human blockade, which was cutting off his only known path to freedom.

"Robert Edward, always use good judgment!" His mother's advice had found this inopportune time to serve as a reminder. His only feasible option was to climb, and so he started up the frail rickety staircase.

In what appeared to be the halfway point in his ascent, the feeble banister offered an ear-splitting screech as it partially gave way. Bobby frantically pawed for the wall and continued in a desperate hand over hand fashion.

Suddenly, without any warning, the door at the foot of the steps opened. Looking down, Bobby saw light rush out of that apartment as if it were suffocating and fighting for fresh air. The silhouette of a petite, haggard old woman presented itself.

She peeked out, looked upward towards him and then she turned to find a hulking figure of a man adjacent to her. She then, in almost an apologetic manner, slowly closed the door.

In that brief moment of light, both hunter and quarry had been able to pinpoint each other. This boogie man was not a mother's machination, nor would he vanish in the daylight; he was real!

"Bobby, Oh Bobby, we're going to have a party!" X's tune reeked of eeriness.

There would be no need to yell for help, not in this hellhole.

"Keep your wits about you!"

"The life you save could be your own!"

"Don't take candy from strangers!"

"Lord, if I ever get out of this one, I'll never, never do..."

All these thoughts had flashed through the ticker tape in his mind. The sweat continued to pour. His thunderous heartbeat had now become his entire head. Bobby's brain may have been addled by an earlier faux pas, but now it was coming up to speed. And so he took to the higher ground by breaking through a door at the top of the staircase.

Light was instantly restored. He found himself in a large room. To the right was a large king-sized bed with large holes through the mattress. What appeared to be strips of rags were knotted on the rungs of the head and foot posts. Above the bed with the shade half drawn was a large window. Outside and below that window was four stories.

This is not an option, Bobby thought to himself. Straight ahead of him was nothing but wall. To the left was another door. Bobby veered left. The door proved to be an entryway to another room with no other exit. There was a small sofa, a coffee table with the picture of a little girl and an old grass bottomed chair with the seat worn through.

There was no booze and no women. *Think, Bobby, think!*

By the time Bobby had retraced his steps back into the larger room, Mr. X had already entered it and was hurriedly locking the door.

"Where's the party man?" queried Bobby, both irritated and ashamed of himself, knowing that he had been duped.

"You're the party, and you're all the party I need." It had delighted X to finally get this charade out of the way. He now looked like the cat that was about to swallow the canary.

Bobby searched for a voice a few octaves lower than normal, "Man this ain't going down like this!"

He could feel his muscles tensing. Lightning fast reflexes carried him over to the door and he had unlocked several of the locks before the astonished X could react. Mr. X rushed over and tried to restrain Bobby. He was met with a right jab followed by a roundhouse kick that jettisoned X across the room. Bobby looked back to see X dribbling down the wall.

"Run fool, run!" Bobby headed towards the stairs. Each step's descent echoed with the sound of freedom's path being cleared. "I don't know where in the hell I am but..." and then inexplicably he froze in the middle of the staircase. Insanity had engulfed him.

His clothes were locked in X's car! Why this fact would even remotely be entertained, and virtually take precedence over life itself, truly defies logic. But there he stood frozen on the steps.

"Oh, I'm so sorry. I thought you were," blurted out X, as he had just stumbled through the door.

"You thought I was what?"

"You know, that way," explained X, "I'll take you back to the campus." The once-brash voice was now meek and filled with apology.

"You're damned straight you will!" shouted Bobby, now seemingly in command. "Let's go!"

As they rode back towards the campus the tension between them was as suffocating as the last breath taken before the floor falls away leaving the rope and the noose to hold its victim's weight. Bobby exhaled. He wondered what had set Mr. X upon this path, and upon his trail? How many others had he duped?

This was not the time for academic curiosity. Bobby had been lucky and that's all it had been – just dumb luck. He also knew that he would never share the memory of this day's near tragedy or its triumph with anyone. No, not even with Ike and certainly not Sheila, whom he already owed and would share one confession.

Looking down Bobby noticed that his right leg was violently trembling. He stomped his foot almost through the floorboard and the trembling stopped.   Terrified by the explosive sound, Mr. X accelerated to sixty-five miles per hour right through the city streets.

We all went to the very same school. We were princes and paupers and so very much like the parents who were trying to raise us. Some of our differences were immediately noticeable like the dapper dressers vs. dungarees or khaki types. There was the latest shoes vs converse sneakers but there was also the studious standouts vs the class clowns.

Seldom were the cries of the clowns that acted out actually listened to and each time they were heard the student was herded to detention, the Principal's office or worse—to a few days of suspension or even eviction.

Education for these children was a failure because the students themselves couldn't or wouldn't communicate to a school system that grew deaf to their deafening cries and presumed them to be retarded.

And so they were held in holding pens designed for the mentally delayed. There they would not be considered a behavioral problem because acting out was the norm and its purpose didn't serve for mental growth, only for time served.

Home for other children was a hot meal, homework and getting ready for tomorrow. Home for many of these children was a fragile fortress held together by that child's working or hustling just to buy groceries midweek to eat and a father's scouring the city for another job that he could find "just to make ends meet."

This was no heroic gesture it was just survival. When the stresses of failure ballooned out of control and burst in that cardboard walled maze called The Projects--they left families in disarray, members mentally hurt or physically battered and some in absentia.

School, it seems was always the next day and this was never discussed in school. It was internalized completely by not talking or partially in concealed snide remarks aimed at the unsuspecting "other kids".

Who studied during a nuclear bomb drill? Certainly not when the spontaneous impromptu unabridged home version lands in your own living room. While in school the very next morning, "Did you have your homework?"

"Nope!"

"The door prize for you then mister, is detention for a week, no for a month, no for a lifetime!".

Then at night, your old man shows up and starts in with his fifth degree, like he was a model student when he himself had dropped out in the sixth grade.

Perhaps now with just a hint of bourbon on his breathe he wants to preach and then pound some good sense into you. Before you know it, you're enduring Hell's torture, while aware that the "other kids" fathers, at the very worse, would only have placed them on television restriction for a week.

Hmmmmm... Perhaps there was a Fourth Boogie Man...

Four: The Death Dance

Fear blanketed Bobby's room like a coastal fog. It was suffocating him. At first his nervous energy had been put to good use as he made up his bed and did his homework. He had even swept the floor.

Now, with nothing else to do, he sat frozen in the chair in his room and waited. What had seemed an eternity ended as a deep voice at the door interrupted the dead silence in the apartment.

His father's voice, even in a whisper, echoed down the hallway like distant thunder. This impending storm was too close to calm him. At twelve years old, he just sat there drew in a deep breath and started to tremble.

Who had ever had a perfect day? A day like that, a day where everything went right? It did not exist in Bobby's world. A few minutes passed and his mother then summoned him to the dinner table.

After a brief blessing over the pork and beans his father started asking questions for which he already knew the answers. He must have talked to mom just before they were seated. Bobby hated these dinners because it always served as an introduction to a card game in which he had the losing hand. The stakes were always too high. Showdown was about to begin:

"Bobby, what did you do today?" his father asked.

A sheepish "Nothing really Dad" was uttered just above a whisper and answers like that always demanded a further explanation.

"Nothing? Did you clean your room?"

"No". (Fear had made him forget). "No, what?"

" No sir, Dad".

" Boy, you better learn how to talk to me."

"Yes sir, Dad".

What happened to your mother's money from the grocery store?"

"Oh William, it was just about twenty cents!"

His mother was trying desperately to defuse a fire that was clearly out of her hands.

"I lost some of it."

And yesterday's homework?"

"I handed it in?"

"But what grade did you get?"

"An F"

"And did you come directly home from school today, like I told you??!!"

"Well, I forgot Dad."

"You forgot??!!"

Bobby's father continued to raise his voice, almost in octaves, as he spoke in a very controlled manner. It was as if he was practicing musical scales, like some baritone, only through clenched teeth. His jaws flaunted muscles that could have been the biceps on any average person.

"Go straight to your room and wait for me. I'll be right back there!"

Bobby reached his room at a sprinter's pace. The time that had elapsed from his father's last words, "right back there," until ... seemed like another eternity or perhaps this was just another long pause from the last one. His fear returned and intensified.

His throat was desert dry and Bobby tried to swallow but a mass the size of his fist prevented him. He could feel his throat swelling and constricting at the same time. His own spit seemed to scratch and cut as he tried again to swallow.

His breathing quickened and became twice as difficult as his heart was pounding so loud and hard that he thought it would burst right through his chest. Clothes were sticking to him as if he'd been swimming in them. Bobby wiped the sweat from his forehead.

The window shade was pulled down in his room and the poorly lit hallway only framed the open doorway leaving Bobby to drown in its airless darkness. His father had always demanded that he stand at attention in the middle of the room like a soldier until he arrived. His legs had tired from standing so long and he resorted to leaning against the bed.

He could feel his fear multiplying and wiped the sweat from his forehead. Bobby's memory had not been addled however as he punished himself over and over again; recalling only two nights ago what again would soon ensue.

After what appeared to be an hour, Bobby figured that surely his dad was trying to psyche him out or had forgotten all together. He wanted to believe the latter.

He changed into his pajamas and then kneeled at the bedside and began to pray. He prayed for a long time too.

"Amen and thank you God for making dad forget." Bobby felt relieved as he eased himself to his feet. He turned towards the poorly-lit hallway and light stared over a huge hulking shadow exposing a wide black leather belt held high to the ceiling.

Quicker than light speed his father grabbed Bobby's arm with his left hand, holding it in a vice-like grip as SHAP, SHAP, SHAP, SHAP, rang out like gunshots. The sound ricocheted from wall to wall and just above the echoes an enraged thunderous voice yelled out over and over again:

"You're going to obey me! You're going to obey me, or I'll kill you!"

A flood of tears trailed the realization of what was occurring only after Bobby's first involuntary screams and leaps, through the white-hot shock of pain.

"Yes, sir Daddy, Yes Sir Daddy, I Will!" he cried out as Bobby began to run in circles. He felt as if blood was running down his legs, with each of his father's savage strokes. Bobby burst into a full gallop, circling like a rogue horse on a carousel. Around and up, gallop, leap and gallop; around and down gallop, dive; gallop were the movements it initiated.

He tried to catch his breath. Spurred on by the encouragement of his dad's powerful and tireless right arm this endless waltz continued in 6/8 time. Each volley of SHAP,

SHAP, SHAP, and SHAP sent out jolts of electricity that cut through his clothes splaying his skin down to the white of the bone from his head to the toes.

"Yes sir, Daddy! Yes sir, Daddy, I promise! Please, Daddy!" Bobby pleaded as he tried to cover himself.

"Daddy, Daddy, I promise to do better! I promise, Daddy!" was the automatic response to the pain, but his father, who must have summoned his strength from some unholy source, had grown deaf in the process.

"Daddy, I'll do better! Please!" were Bobby's last words, his shrill cries in time weakened to a whisper, and then he was silent. His father continued to exact his anger on the child, from head to toe, and then back again until Bobby finally fell to the floor.

There would be no more tears – they had been completely exhausted. Bobby's mouth was wide open and, although the dried blood about his cracked lips wasn't chocking him, air refused to rush in or out.

Whether he had mustered his last ounce of strength to get to his feet again or his father had hoisted him up, Robert Banks was now too weak to stand or even move and he fell back to the floor vulnerable; still his father showered him with a hundred thousand more volts of pain.

That wide black belt continuously found its destination. It's shrill SHAP, SHAP, SHAP, SHAP sound echoed from body to wall, penetrating through into the next room bringing no response from the recipient. Bobby's mother wept aloud but her cries could not be heard. She felt every vicious lash herself and recoiled in anticipation of the next.

It had never helped for her to try and intervene; in fact, it only seemed to make things worse. She prayed that this would quickly run its course but had no idea how far it was from the start or end of its eternity.

The carousel now teetered to a standstill with its rogue horse now beaten and broken – and still the beating continued. Bobby 's body refused to hurt any more. His nerves were without reflexes, but his father continued on with his belt hand, still dedicated to its task.

There was no more pain because pain had become yesterday's servant. Bobby now distant from himself, sat in the farthest corner of his room and watched. He was almost apathetic about this massacre as the predator finally crushed the windpipe of his prey.

With his victim now completely lifeless Willie Banks drew back his weapon through its belt looped scabbard and retired from his son's room.

Like the end of a great storm, this hulking shadow gradually receded down the hallway as its voice heaved, "You're going to obey me! You're going to obey me."

The echoing thunder reverberated off into the distance, while in disaster's wake, Bobby watched himself lay lifeless on the floor. He wondered if he was truly dead, and if not, would he return to this tattered form or be freer without it? Suddenly, he felt himself sigh and heard his own whimpering once again.

www.ingramcontent.com/pod-product-compliance
Lightning Source LLC
Chambersburg PA
CBHW031904170626
46807CB00004B/1882